FRASER

D1507924

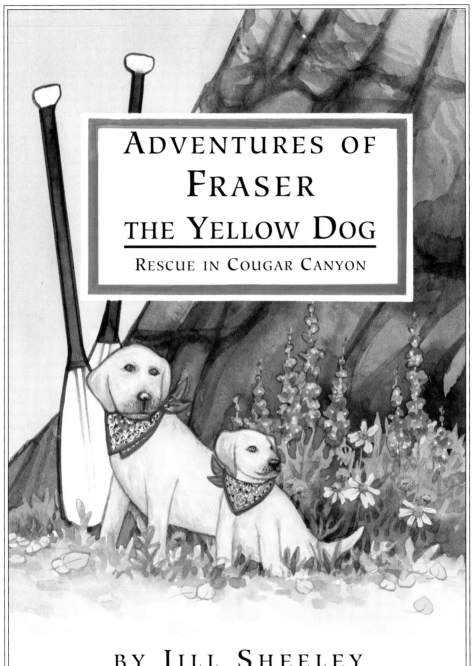

ADVENTURES OF
FRASER
THE YELLOW DOG
RESCUE IN COUGAR CANYON

BY JILL SHEELEY

ILLUSTRATED BY TAMMIE LANE

COURTNEY PRESS

First edition published in 2004 by Courtney Press, Aspen, Colorado
Copyright © 2004 by Jill Sheeley

A very special thanks to Rob Seideman, Tammie Lane, Bob Jenkins, Bob Harris, Callie
Long, my family and all my many friends who gave me advice and support.

This is a fictional story. The girls, Fraser and Maggie go rafting "alone" in this story for the
sake of adventure. In real life, the author recommends rafting with a qualified guide.

For more information about ordering this book, write: Jill Sheeley • P.O. Box 845 • Aspen,
CO 81612. Check out our website: www.jillsheeleybooks.com

Printed in Korea
ISBN 0-9609108-8-3

Mail us your rescue stories to: Jill Sheeley • P.O. Box 845 • Aspen, CO 81612.

Visit us on the web at www.jillsheeleybooks.com

This book is dedicated to Sara McFlynn and Robbie Wade — two Aspen teens who passed away in the summer of 2002 in two separate tragedies. They were both amazing: talented, high-spirited and adventuresome. Their smiles lit up a room. They would have loved going on this rafting adventure. Now, they remain in our hearts forever.

Partial Proceeds from this book will benefit Sopris Therapy Services – an incredible non-profit program in the Aspen area that promotes the health and quality of life for the disabled through equine assisted therapy. www.sopristherapyservices.com

Courtney, Katy and Taylor love to drink Fiji Water. It's the best tasting, purest, natural water available from the Fiji Islands. For more information about this healthy drink, contact Fiji at 877-H2O-FIJI (426-3454) or check out their website at: www.fijiwater.com

Maggie is wearing an NRS life preserver in this rafting adventure. It's commonly known as a canine floatation device - C.F.D. After all, some dogs jump in the water and others fall in. The NRS C.F.D. keeps them on the surface. Fraser and Maggie love water sports and use their NRS jackets often. For more information on this comfortable jacket, contact NRS on the web at: www.nrs.com

Special thanks to the Iams Co. for making high quality, nutritious foods for Fraser, Maggie and millions of other dogs around the world. Check out our website: www.iams.com

Courtney, Katy and Taylor are "happy campers" with their versatile Marmot sleeping bags and tent. For more information on Marmot products, contact them at: www.marmot.com

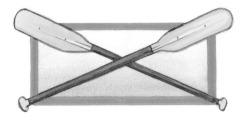

I love slumber parties," said Taylor.

"Me too," said Katy, "but if I don't get to sleep soon, I won't be much help paddling tomorrow."

"I'm going to wake up before anyone, and bake us a treat,"said Courtney. "I can't wait to get back on the river, but boy am I scared about Cougar Falls."

"Good night, Fraser," said Taylor.

"Good night, Maggie," said Katy.

"Good night, everyone," said Courtney.

"Good morning, good morning," said Courtney, offering her just-baked banana muffins with melted butter. "Let's get to work!"

The girls loaded their mountain bikes and shouted out a check list.

"Courtney," said Taylor, "it's so cool that your dad loaned us Magic."

"Do you think it's a strong enough raft to get us over Cougar Falls?" asked Katy.

"I doubt it'll be a magic carpet ride," said Taylor laughing.

"Let's boogie," said Courtney.

"Oh what a beautiful morning, oh what a beautiful day...," sang the girls.

Fraser and Maggie ran alongside the girls, occasionally stopping to play with a stick. The golden aspen leaves smelled like carnations.

"OK," said Taylor, "I think we have the last item loaded."

Fraser and Maggie were running back and forth in the raft.

"I know you're excited," laughed Courtney. "I am too!"

The girls set off at a leisurely pace. Tomorrow there was Cougar Falls to contend with. Today there was nothing to do but enjoy the river. It sparkled like diamonds in the sun, and lapped at its sandy banks. The gentle river was peaceful.

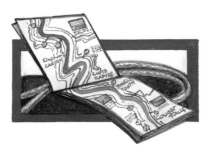

"I can't wait to try out our new Marmot tent and sleeping bags," said Taylor.

"How many lawns did we mow to earn the money?" asked Katy.

"Who cares," said Courtney, "just think how cozy we'll be tonight!"

"I just hope we don't see any bears," said Katy.

"No problem," said Courtney, "Fraser and Maggie will scare them away. All we have to worry about is getting our food up a tree, so the bears can't reach it."

"BRRRRRR," said Courtney, "the water's as cold as ice."

"Let's eat," said Taylor, "I'm hungry as a bear. Hot dogs and chips - YUM!"

"This river map is amazing," said Katy. "We're right here."

"Cool," said Taylor, "do you see Snaggle Tooth rapids? We'll be hitting them after lunch."

"They're a mile away," said Katy, "and they're only Class II rapids. Should be a piece of cake."

"Let's be calm and work together like we practiced," said Courtney.

"I see Snaggle Tooth up ahead," said Taylor.
"Paddle, paddle!" yelled Courtney.
"Yippee," screamed Taylor.
"Yahoo," shouted Courtney and Katy.
The girls were all smiles as Magic rode Snaggle Tooth's swells and crashed over the tops of breaking waves. They shot right down the center, free falling.
"That was awesome!" cried Taylor.
"What a blast!" laughed Katy.

The girls arrived at Black Bear Island in the late afternoon.

"I'll set the tent up," said Courtney.

"I'll unpack the dry bags," offered Katy. "But let's hurry, so we can play Frisbee!"

"Hey look," said Taylor, "Fraser's found dinner!"

"Let's go fishing," said Courtney.

"I love this campsite," said Taylor, "I wish we could stay here forever."

"Me too," said Katy, "but I'm so tired and I can't stop worrying about Cougar Falls tomorrow. They say it'll eat you alive."

"We'll be fine, Katy," said Courtney confidently, although fear rose in her throat as she thought about the dangerous rooster tails and the dreaded Ragged Rock of Cougar Falls.

The girls became quiet and listened to the hoot of an owl, the click of bats overhead, and a beaver slapping its tail.

Soon everyone fell sound asleep.

"Oh no," cried Courtney. "Trouble. Big trouble."

"I can't believe it," said Katy. "We must have been so tired, we didn't hear them. Those tricky bears! They clawed our raft."

"I guess we can't blame the bears," said Courtney. "We must have left a candy bar in the raft."

"At least they didn't get our food," said Taylor.

"Now what?" asked Katy.

"We'll use our trusty patch kit and pump," said Courtney, "and repair Magic. We know how."

"How will we handle Cougar Falls now?" asked Katy.

"I guess we'll never know until we try," said Courtney. "No guts, no glory."

The girls loaded their gear and shoved off. They stopped at the next bank so they could scout Cougar Falls.

"Oh my gosh," said Katy, "no wonder it's rated Class IV. Just look at Ragged Rock."

"I can hear my heart pounding," said Courtney.

"My knees are shaking," added Katy.

"Let's go for it!" said Taylor.

The girls pulled out and followed the bubble line into the tongue of Cougar Falls. Courtney had to yell over the roar of the river which sounded like a locomotive.

"Don't hit Ragged Rock. It's wicked."

"Paddle! paddle!!!" screamed Taylor.

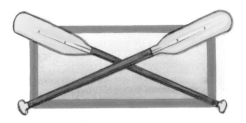

"It's sucking us right to it," yelled Courtney.

Speeding fast and out of control, Magic hit the side of Ragged Rock as a blast of water hit them violently, spinning them sideways. The roar of the river was deafening.

Katy and Taylor were a tangled, mangled mass on the bottom of the raft. Courtney was thrown overboard like a rag doll, disappearing and reappearing from within spitting, foaming, bubbling rapids.

"Oh Maggie," cried Courtney shivering. "I hope Katy, Taylor and Fraser are okay. I don't know where they are. I don't even know where we are. Should we stay put?...should we go looking for them?...what's the right thing to do?"

Maggie lifted her head and licked away Courtney's tears. She pulled the zipper on Courtney's life preserver with her sharp teeth.

"You're so smart, Maggie, I forgot all about the waterproof matches. We can build a fire and warm up."

"It's okay, Maggie," Courtney said, "everything's going to be all right."

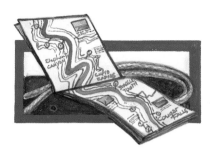

"Hey boy," cried Courtney, "You're okay! Are Katy and Taylor okay, too? Do you know where they are?"

Fraser grabbed Courtney by the arm and started pulling her. Maggie joined in and tugged Courtney's ankle.

Courtney laughed, "Looks like you two know something I don't. OK, OK, I'll follow you, Fraser."

As Courtney did her best to keep up with Fraser and Maggie, the dogs barked incessantly.

"We're here!" yelled Taylor. "We're over here."

"Fraser found us," Courtney explained when she reached camp.

"He saved our lives," Taylor said. "Fraser pulled us to shore. Lucky for us, the raft got tangled by the logs in the eddy."

"We were so scared the falls swept you and Maggie away," said Katy.

"Fraser took off running," said Taylor. "We figured he must have caught your scent."

"I'm so happy we're all together safe and sound," said Courtney. "My dogs saved the day! We can spend our last night here. Tomorrow will be an easy float to the take-out."

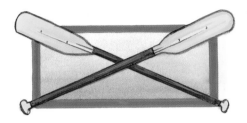

"Are we ever glad to see you," smiled River Ranger Bob. "This morning we found this life preserver floating down the river and worried that someone was in trouble."

The girls looked at each other. "You might say we were," laughed Courtney.

She hugged Fraser and said, "I think Maggie deserves to come on our next adventure. Don't you?"

Rafting Tips

River rafting is a wonderful sport. Preparation and proper instruction by an expert guide are required. Always be prepared for the worse-case scenario. Following are a few things to know when going on a raft trip:

- ❏ Always wear an approved life jacket
- ❏ Wear correct footwear with no socks
- ❏ Keep both legs in the raft
- ❏ Always listen to your guide or designated leader
- ❏ If you fall out of the raft, float on your back with your feet downstream
- ❏ Wear sunscreen and a hat or visor
- ❏ Drink plenty of water (not river water)
- ❏ Be prepared for all kinds of weather
- ❏ Stay together
- ❏ Have a plan, carry a river map
- ❏ Don't wear cotton
- ❏ Take only pictures — leave only footprints